PLAYDATE PALS

HAMSTER
LEARNS TO
HELP

Rosie Greening • Dawn Machell

make
believe
ideas

One day, the animals were tidying up after playing.

There was a lot to do,
but **Hamster** wasn't **helping**.

Puppy was carrying a big pile of bricks to the toy box.

"**Hamster**, please can you **help** me?" asked Puppy.

"No, I want to do a jigsaw puzzle," said **Hamster**.

Squirrel was putting clothes
back in the dressing-up box.

"**Hamster**, please can you **help** me?"
asked Squirrel.

"No, I'm doing my jigsaw puzzle,"
said **Hamster**.

Bear was taking books back to the bookshelf.

"**Hamster**, please can you **help** me?"
asked Bear.

"No, I'm still doing my jigsaw puzzle,"
said **Hamster**.

Soon, there was just one piece
missing from the puzzle.

Hamster looked in the box,
but there was nothing there!

She asked her friends if they could **help** her look.

"We're too busy!" they said, and they carried on tidying.

So **Hamster** tried to find
the puzzle piece on her own.

She looked around, but she couldn't
see the piece anywhere!

Bear told **Hamster**, "If you **help** us tidy up, the jobs will be finished quickly.

Then we can all look for the missing piece **together**!"

So **Hamster** started to **help**.

Hamster worked very hard.
She picked up bricks . . .

and put away
dressing-up clothes . . .

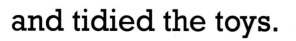

and tidied the toys.

"Well done, **Hamster**!" said Squirrel.

Hamster smiled. She felt **good** for **helping** out.

With **Hamster's** help, the tidying was soon finished so the friends searched for the missing piece **together**.

Squirrel lifted up the rug ...
and the missing piece was underneath!

"**Thank you**, Squirrel!" said **Hamster**,
and she rushed to complete her puzzle.

Hamster was glad that she had such **helpful** friends.

"Let's do the next puzzle **together**!" suggested **Hamster**.

It was the perfect reward for their hard work!

READING TOGETHER

Playdate Pals have been written for parents, carers and teachers to share with young children who are beginning to explore the feelings they have about themselves and the world around them.

Each story is intended as a springboard to emotional discovery and can be used to gently promote further discussion around the feeling or behavioural topic featured in the book.

Hamster Learns to Help is designed to help children learn that a willingness to help is an important part of developing social relationships. Once you have read the story together, go back and talk about any experiences the children might share with Hamster. Talk to children about helping and then encourage them to do so in other trusted relationships.

Look at the pictures

Talk about the characters. Do they look happy when Hamster doesn't help? What about when she does help? Help children think about how helping affects others.

Words in bold

Throughout each story there are words highlighted in bold type. These words specify either the **character's name** or useful words and phrases relating to **helping.** You may wish to put emphasis on these words or use them as reminders for parts of the story you can return to and discuss.

Questions you can ask

To prompt further exploration of this behavioural topic, you could try asking children some of the following questions:

- How do you feel when people help you?
- What should you say if someone helps you?
- Can you think of a way to help someone?
- What is good about helping?